*1972*

# LIKE
# A BULWARK

# LIKE
# A BULWARK

By Marianne Moore

The Viking Press · NEW YORK · 1957

Acknowledgment is made to magazines here specified, as well as
to the editors who published this verse and, in the instance of
"Tom Fool" and "The Staff of Aesculapius," much improved it:

"Bulwarked against Fate" (originally entitled "At Rest in the
Blast"); requested by William Rose Benét, *The Saturday Review
of Literature*, March 19, 1949. "Apparition of Splendor"; Mar-
garet Marshall, *The Nation*, October 25, 1952. "Then the Er-
mine"; Nicholas Joost, *Poetry, A Magazine of Verse*, October
1952. "Tom Fool at Jamaica"; Mrs. E. B. White, *The New
Yorker*, June 13, 1953 (commissioned originally for use elsewhere
by Robert Offergeld). "The Web One Weaves of Italy"; Alan
Pryce-Jones, *The Times Literary Supplement*, London, September 17, 1954. "The Staff of Aesculapius"; Joseph S. Dunham,
*What's New*, Abbott Laboratories, December 1954. "The Syca-
more"; Thomas B. Hess, *The Art News Annual*, 1955. "Rosemary"; Allene Talmey, *Vogue*, December 1954. "Style"; the
greater part published by *The Listener*, April 12, 1956. "Logic
and 'The Magic Flute'"; Edward M. Hood, *Shenandoah*, Sum-
mer 1956. "Blessed is the Man"; signalizing the Class Day cere-
monies of the Columbia University Chapter of Phi Beta Kappa,
June 4, 1956; Elizabeth McFarland, *The Ladies' Home Journal*,
August 1956.

# CONTENTS

# Bulwarked against Fate

Affirmed. Pent by power that holds it fast —
a paradox. Pent. Hard pressed,
    you take the blame and are inviolate.
        Abased at last;
        not the tempest-tossed.
Compressed; firmed by the thrust of the blast
    till compact, like a bulwark against fate;
        lead-saluted,
        saluted by lead?
As though flying Old Glory full mast.

# Apparition of Splendor

Partaking of the miraculous
    since never known literally,
Dürer's rhinoceros
    might have startled us equally
    if black-and-white-spined elaborately.

Like another porcupine, or fern,
    the mouth in an arching egret
was too black to discern
    till exposed as a silhouette;
    but the double-embattled thistle of jet —

disadvantageous supposedly —
    has never shot a quill. Was it
some joyous fantasy,
    plain eider-eared exhibit
    of spines rooted in the sooty moss,

or "train supported by porcupines —
    a fairy's eleven yards long"? ...
as when the lightning shines
    on thistlefine spears, among
    prongs in lanes above lanes of a shorter prong,

"with the forest for nurse," also dark
        at the base — where needle-debris
springs and shows no footmark;
        the setting for a symmetry
        you must not touch unless you are a fairy.

Maine should be pleased that its animal
        is not a waverer, and rather
than fight, lets the primed quill fall.
        Shallow oppressor, intruder,
        insister, you have found a resister.

9

# Then the Ermine:

"rather dead than spotted"; and believe it
     despite reason to think not,
I saw a bat by daylight;
hard to credit

but I knew that I was right. It charmed me —
     wavering like a jack-in-
the-green, weaving about me
insecurely.

Instead of hammer-handed bravado
     adopting force for fashion,
momentum with a motto:
*Mutare sperno*

*vel timere* — I don't change, am not craven;
     although on what ground could I
say that I am hard to frighten?
Nothing's certain.

Fail, and Lavater's physiography
     has another admirer
of skill in obscurity —
now a novelty.

So let the *palisandre* settee express
　　change, "ebony violet,"
Master Corbo in full dress,
and shepherdess,

at once; exhilarating hoarse crow-note
　　and dignity with intimacy.
Foiled explosiveness is yet
a kind of prophet,

a perfecter, and so a concealer —
　　with the power of implosion;
like violets by Dürer;
even darker.

# Tom Fool at Jamaica

Look at Jonah embarking from Joppa, deterred by
the whale; hard going for a statesman whom nothing
could detain,
although one who would not rather die than repent.
Be infallible at your peril, for your system will fail,
and select as a model the schoolboy in Spain
who at the age of six, portrayed a mule and jockey
who had pulled up for a snail.

"There is submerged magnificence, as Victor Hugo
said." *Sentir avec ardeur;* that's it; magnetized by feeling.
Tom Fool "makes an effort and makes it oftener
than the rest" — out on April first, a day of some
significance
in the ambiguous sense — the smiling
Master Atkinson's choice, with that mark of a
champion, the extra
spurt when needed. Yes, yes. "Chance

is a regrettable impurity"; like Tom Fool's
left white hind foot — an unconformity; though
judging by
results, a kind of cottontail to give him confidence.
Up in the cupola comparing speeds, Signor Capossela
keeps his head.

"It's tough," he said; "but I get 'em; and why shouldn't I?
I'm relaxed, I'm confident, and I don't bet." Sensa-
                                                        tional. He does not
        bet on his animated


valentines — his pink and black-striped, sashed or
                                                dotted silks.
Tom Fool is "a handy horse," with a chiseled foot. You've
                                                the beat
        of a dancer to a measure or harmonious rush
        of a porpoise at the prow where the racers all win
                                        easily —
like centaurs' legs in tune, as when kettledrums compete;
nose rigid and suede nostrils spread, a light left hand
                                        on the rein, till
        well — this is a rhapsody.


Of course, speaking of champions, there was
                                        Fats Waller
with the feather touch, giraffe eyes, and that hand
                                        alighting in
        Ain't Misbehavin'! Ozzie Smith and Eubie Blake
        ennoble the atmosphere; you recall the
                                        Lippizan school;
the time Ted Atkinson charged by on Tiger Skin —
no pursuers in sight — cat-loping along. And you
                                may have seen a monkey
        on a greyhound. "But Tom Fool . . .


13

# The Web One Weaves of Italy

grows till it is not what but which,
blurred by too much. The very blasé alone could
      choose the contest or fair to which to go.
      The crossbow tournament at Gubbio?

For quiet excitement, canoe-ers
or peach fairs? or near Perugia, the mule-show;
      if not the Palio, slaying the Saracen.
      One salutes — on reviewing again

this modern *mythologica*
*esopica* — its nonchalances of the mind,
      that "fount by which enchanting gems are spilt."
      And are we not charmed by the result? —

quite different from what goes on
at the Sorbonne; but not entirely, since flowering
      in more than mere talent for spectacle.
      Because the heart is in it all is well.


Note: The greater part of stanzas 1 and 2 is quoted from an article
by Mitchell Goodman, "Festivals and Fairs for the Tourist in
Italy," *New York Times*, April 18, 1954.

# The Staff of Aesculapius

A symbol from the first, of mastery,
    experiments such as Hippocrates made
        and substituted for vague
    speculation, stayed
        the ravages of a plague.

A "going on"; yes, *anastasis* is the word
    for research a virus has defied,
        and for the virologist
    with variables still untried —
        too impassioned to desist.

Suppose that research has hit on the right one
    and a killed vaccine is effective
        say temporarily —
    for even a year — although a live
        one could give lifelong immunity,

knowledge has been gained for another attack.
    Selective injury to cancer
        cells without injury to
    normal ones — another
        gain — looks like prophecy come true.

Now, after lung resection, the surgeon fills space.
To sponge implanted, cells following
fluid, adhere and what
was inert becomes living —
that was framework. Is it not

like the master-physician's Sumerian rod? —
staff and effigy of the animal
which by shedding its skin
is a sign of renewal —
the symbol of medicine.

# The Sycamore

> Against a gun-metal sky
> I saw an albino giraffe. Without
> leaves to modify,
chamois-white as
said, though partly pied near the base,
> it towered where a chain of
> > stepping-stones lay in a stream nearby;
> > glamour to stir the envy

> of anything in motley —
> Hampshire pig, the living lucky-stone; or
> all-white butterfly.
A commonplace:
there's more than just one kind of grace.
> We don't like flowers that do
> > not wilt; they must die, and nine
> > she-camel-hairs aid memory.

> Worthy of Imami,
> the Persian — clinging to a stiffer stalk
> was a little dry
thing from the grass,
in the shape of a Maltese cross,
> retiringly formal
> > as if to say: "And there was I
> > like a field-mouse at Versailles."

17

# Rosemary

Beauty and Beauty's son and rosemary —
Venus and Love, her son, to speak plainly —
born of the sea supposedly,
at Christmas each, in company,
braids a garland of festivity.
    Not always rosemary —

since the flight to Egypt, blooming differently.
With lancelike leaf, green but silver underneath,
its flowers — white originally —
turned blue. The herb of memory,
imitating the blue robe of Mary,
    is not too legendary

to flower both as symbol and as pungency.
Springing from stones beside the sea,
the height of Christ when thirty-three —
not higher — it feeds on dew and to the bee
"hath a dumb language"; is in reality
    a kind of Christmas-tree.

# Style

revives in Escudero's constant of the plumbline,
axis of the hairfine moon — his counter-camber of
                                          the skater.
No more fanatical adjuster
            of the tilted hat
than Escudero; of tempos others can't combine.
            And we — besides evolving
      the classic silhouette, Dick Button whittled
                                    slender —


have an Iberian-American champion yet,
the deadly Etchebaster. Entranced, were you not,
                              by Soledad?
black-clad solitude that is not sad;
            like a letter from
      Casals; or perhaps say literal alphabet-
            S soundholes in a 'cello
      set contradictorily; or should we call her


*la lagarta?* or bamboos with fireflies a-glitter;
or glassy lake and the whorls which a vertical stroke
                              brought about,
of the paddle half-turned coming out.
            As if bisecting

19

a viper, she can dart down three times and recover
without a disaster, having
been a bull-fighter. Well; she has a forgiver.

Etchebaster's art, his catlike ease, his mousing pose,
his genius for anticipatory tactics, preclude envy
as the traditional unwavy
Sandeman sailor
is Escudero's; the guitar, Rosario's —
wrist-rest for a dangling hand
that's suddenly set humming fast fast fast
and faster.

There is no suitable simile. It is as though
the equidistant three tiny arcs of seeds in a banana
had been conjoined by Palestrina;
it is like the eyes,
or say the face, of Palestrina by El Greco.
O Escudero, Soledad,
Rosario Escudero, Etchebaster!

# Logic and "The Magic Flute"

Up winding stair,
here, where, in what theatre lost?
was I seeing a ghost —
a reminder at least
    of a sunbeam or moonbeam
that has not a waist?
    By hasty hop
    or accomplished mishap,
the magic flute and harp
somehow confused themselves
    with China's precious wentletrap.

    Near Life and Time
in their peculiar catacomb,
abalonean gloom
and an intrusive hum
    pervaded the mammoth cast's
small audience-room.
    Then out of doors,
    where interlacing pairs
of skaters raced from rink
to ramp, a demon roared
    as if down flights of marble stairs:

    " 'What is love and
shall I ever have it?'" The truth

is simple. Banish sloth,
fetter-feigning uncouth
    fraud. Trapper Love with noble
noise, the magic sleuth,
    as bird-notes prove —
    first telecolor-trove —
illogically wove
what logic can't unweave:
    you need not shoulder, need not shove.

# Blessed is the Man

who does not sit in the seat of the scoffer —
  the man who does not denigrate, depreciate,
                          denunciate;
    who is not "characteristically intemperate,"
  who does not "excuse, retreat, equivocate; and will
                          be heard."

(Ah, Giorgione! there are those who mongrelize
  and those who heighten anything they touch;
                          although it may well be
    that if Giorgione's self-portrait were not said to be he,
  it might not take my fancy. Blessed the geniuses who
                          know

that egomania is not a duty.)
  "Diversity, controversy; tolerance" — in that "citadel
    of learning" we have a fort that ought to armor us
                          well.
  Blessed is the man who "takes the risk of a decision," —
                          asks

himself the question: "Would it solve the problem?
  Is it right as I see it? Is it in the best interests of all?"
    Alas. Ulysses' companions are now political —
  living self-indulgently until the moral sense is drowned,

23

having lost all power of comparison,
thinking license emancipates one, "slaves whom they
themselves have bound."
Brazen authors, downright soiled and downright
spoiled, as if sound
and exceptional, are the old quasi-modish counterfeit,

Mitin-proofing conscience against character.
Affronted by "private lies and public shame,"
blessed is the author
who favors what the supercilious do not favor —
who will not comply. Blessed, the unaccommodating
man.

Blessed is the man whose faith is different
from possessiveness — of a kind not framed by "things
which do appear" —
who will not visualize defeat, too intent to cower;
whose illumined eye has seen the shaft that gilds the
sultan's tower.

# Notes

*(A poem title becomes line 1 when part of the first sentence.)*

## Apparition of Splendor (page 8)

Lines 16-17: *"train . . . long."* Oliver Goldsmith in one of his essays refers to "a blue fairy with a train eleven yards long, supported by porcupines."

Line 21: *"with . . . nurse."* "All over spines, with the forest for nurse." "The Hedgehog, the Fox, and the Flies," Book Twelve, Fable XIII, *The Fables of La Fontaine* (New York: The Viking Press, 1954).

## Then the Ermine: (page 10)

Line 2: *"rather . . . spotted."* Clitophon; "his device was the Ermion, with a speech that signified, Rather dead than spotted." Sidney's *Arcadia*, Book I, Chapter 17, paragraph 4. Cambridge Classics, Volume I, 1912; edited by Albert Feuillerat.

Line 12: *motto.* Motto of Henry, Duke of Beaufort: *Mutare vel timere sperno.*

Line 18: *Lavater.* John Kaspar Lavater (1741-1801), a student of physiography. His system includes morphological, anthropological, anatomical, histrionical, and graphical studies. Kurt Seligmann: *The Mirror of Magic* (New York: Pantheon Books, 1948, page 332).

25

# Tom Fool at Jamaica (page 12)

Line 6: *mule and jockey*. A mule and jockey by "Giulio Gomez 6 años" from a collection of drawings by Spanish school children, solicited on behalf of a fund-raising committee for Republican Spain, sold by Lord and Taylor; given to me by Miss Louise Crane.

Lines 8-9: *"There . . . said."* The Reverend David C. Shipley, July 20, 1952.

Line 9: *Sentir avec ardeur*. By Madame Boufflers—Marie Françoise-Catherine de Beauveau, Marquise de Boufflers (1711-1786). See note by Dr. Achilles Fang, annotating Lu Chi's "Wên Fu" (A.D. 261-303) — his "Rhymeprose on Literature" ("rhymeprose" from "Reimprosa" of German medievalists): "As far as notes go, I am at one with a contemporary of Rousseau's: 'Il faut dire en deux mots / Ce qu'on veut dire'; . . . But I cannot claim 'J'ai réussi,' especially because I broke Mme. de Boufflers' injunction ('Il faut éviter l'emploi / Du moi, du moi.')" *Harvard Journal of Asiatic Studies*, Volume 14, Number 3, December 1951, page 529 (revised, *New Mexico Quarterly*, September 1952).

Air: *Sentir avec ardeur*

Il faut dire en deux mots
Ce qu'on veut dire;
Les longs propos
Sont sots.

Il faut savoir lire
Avant que d'écrire,
Et puis dire en deux mots
Ce qu'on veut dire.
Les longs propos
Sont sots.

Il ne faut pas toujours conter,
Citer,
Dater,
Mais écouter.
Il faut éviter l'emploi
Du moi, du moi,
Voici pourquoi:

Il est tyrannique,
Trop académique;
L'ennui, l'ennui
Marche avec lui.
Je me conduis toujours ainsi
Ici,
Aussi
J'ai réussi.

Il faut dire en deux mots
Ce qu'on veut dire;
Les longs propos
Sont sots.

Line 13: *Master Atkinson.* I opened *The New York Times* one morning (March 3, 1952) and a column by Arthur Daley on Ted Atkinson and Tom Fool took my fancy. Asked what he thought of Hill Gail, Ted Atkinson said, "He's a real good horse, . . . real good," and paused a moment. "But I think he ranks only second to Tom Fool. . . . I prefer Tom Fool. . . . He makes a more sustained effort and makes it more often." Reminded that Citation could make eight or ten spurts in a race, "That's it," said Ted enthusiastically. "It's the mark of a champion to spurt 100 yards, settle back and spurt another 100 yards, giving that extra burst whenever needed. From what I've seen of Tom Fool, I'd call him a 'handy horse.'" He mentioned two others "They had only one way of running. But Tom Fool. . . ." Then I saw a picture of Tom Fool (*New York Times,* April 1, 1952) with Ted Atkinson in the saddle and felt I must pay him a slight tribute; got on with it a little way, then realized that I had just received an award from Youth United for a Better Tomorrow and was worried indeed. I deplore gambling and had never seen a race. Then in the *Times* for July 24, 1952, I saw a column by Joseph C. Nichols about Frederic Capossela, the announcer at Belmont Park, who said when interviewed, "Nervous? No, I'm never nervous. . . . I'll tell you where it's tough. The straightaway at Belmont Park, where as many as twenty-eight horses run at you from a point three quarters of a mile away. I get 'em though, and why shouldn't I? I'm relaxed, I'm confident and I don't bet."

In the way of a sequel, "Money Isn't Everything" by Arthur Daley (*New York Times,* March 1, 1955): "'There's a constant fascination to thoroughbreds,' said Ted, '. . . they're so much like people. . . . My first love was Red Hay . . . a stouthearted little fellow . . . he always tried, always gave his best.' [Mr. Daley: 'The same description fits Atkinson.'] 'There was Devil Diver, . . . the mare Snow Goose. One of my big favorites . . . crazy to get going. . . . But once she swung into stride . . . you could ride her with shoelaces for reins. . . . And then there was Coaltown. . . . There were others of course, but I never met one who could compare with Tom Fool, my favorite of favorites. He had the most personality of all. . . . Just to look at him lit a spark. He had an intelligent head, an intelligent look and, best of all, was intelligent. He had soft eyes, a wide brow and — gee, I'm sounding like a lovesick boy. But I think he had the handsomest face of any horse I ever had anything to do with. He was a great horse but I was fond of him not so much for what he achieved as for what he was.' With that the sprightly Master Theodore fastened the number plate on his right shoulder and headed for the paddock."

Lines 14-15: *"Chance . . . impurity."* The *I Ching* or *Book of Changes*, translated by Richard Wilhelm and Cary Baynes, Bollingen Series XIX (New York: Pantheon Books, 1950).

Line 29: *Fats Waller.* Thomas Waller, "a protean jazz figure," died in 1943. See *The New York Times*, article and Richard Tucker (Pix) photograph, March 16, 1952.

Line 31: *Ozzie Smith.* Osborne Smith, a Negro chanter and drummer who improvised the music of Ian Hugo's *Ai-yé*.

Line 31: *Eubie Blake.* The Negro pianist in *Shuffle Along*.

## The Web One Weaves of Italy (page 14)

Line 12: *"fount . . . spilt."* "The Monkey and the Leopard," Book Nine, Fable III, *The Fables of La Fontaine* (The Viking Press, 1954).

## The Staff of Aesculapius (page 15)

Line 11: *Suppose . . . one. Time*, March 29, 1954, article on the Salk vaccine.

Lines 17-20: *Selective . . . true.* Sloan-Kettering Institute for Cancer Research, *Progress Report VII*, June 1954; pp. 20-21.

Lines 22-25: *To . . . framework.* Abbott Laboratories, "Plastic Sponge Implants in Surgery," *What's New*, Number 186, Christmas 1954.

## The Sycamore (page 17)

Lines 15-16: *nine . . . hairs.* Imami, the Iranian miniaturist, draws "with a brush made of nine hairs from a newborn she camel and a pencil sharpened to a needle's point. . . . He was decorated twice by the late Riza Shah; once for his miniatures and once for his rugs." *New York Times,* March 5, 1954.

## Rosemary (page 18)

Line 17: "*hath . . . language.*" Sir Thomas More (see below).

According to a Spanish legend, rosemary flowers — originally white — turned blue when the Virgin threw her cloak over a rosemary bush, while resting on the flight into Egypt. There is in Trinity College Library, Cambridge, a manuscript sent to Queen Philippa of Hainault by her mother, written by "a clerk of the school of Salerno" and translated by "danyel bain." The manuscript is devoted entirely to the virtues of rosemary, which, we are told, never grows higher than the height of Christ; after thirty-three years the plant increases in breadth but not in height. See "Rosemary of Plesant Savour," by Eleanor Sinclair Rohde, *The Spectator,* July 7, 1930.

## Style (page 19)

Line 8: *Dick Button.* See photograph, *New York Times,* January 2, 1956.

Line 10: *Etchebaster.* Pierre Etchebaster, a machine-gunner in the First World War; champion of France in chistera (jai alai), pala, and mainnues. He took up court tennis in 1922, won the American championship in 1928, and retired in 1954. (*New York Times,* February 13, 1954 and February 24, 1955.) *New York Times,* January 19, 1956: "Pierre Etchebaster, retired world champion, and Frederick S. Moseley won the pro-amateur handicap court tennis tournament at the Racquet

30

and Tennis Club yesterday. . . . The score was 5-6, 6-5, 6-5. Moseley, president of the club, scored the last point of the match with a railroad ace. Johnson and McClintock had pulled up from 3-5 to 5-all in this final set."

Line 10: *Soledad.* Danced in America, 1950-1951.

Line 27: *Rosario's.* Rosario Escudero, one of the company of Vincente Escudero, but not related to him.


## Logic and "The Magic Flute" (page 21)

*The Magic Flute.* Colorcast by NBC Opera Theater, January 15, 1956.

Line 11: *precious wentletrap. n.* [D. *wenteltrap* a winding staircase; cf. G. *wendeltreppe.*] The shell of *E. pretiosa,* of the genus *Epitonium. — Webster's New International Dictionary.*

Lines 23-24: "*"What . . . it?"" Demon in Love* by Horatio Colony (Cambridge, Massachusetts: Hampshire Press, 1955).

Line 25: *Banish sloth.* "Banish sloth; you have defeated Cupid's bow," Ovid, *Remedia Amoris.*

# Blessed is the Man (page 23)

Lines 1-2: *Blessed . . . scoffer.* Psalm 1:1.

Line 4: *"characteristically intemperate."* Campaign manager's evaluation of an attack on the Eisenhower Administration.

Line 5: *"excuse . . . heard."* Charles Poore reviewing James B. Conant's *The Citadel of Learning* (New Haven: Yale University Press) — quoting Lincoln. *New York Times*, April 7, 1956.

Line 8: *Giorgione's self-portrait.* Reproduced in *Life*, October 24, 1955.

Lines 11-12: *"Diversity . . . learning."* James B. Conant, *The Citadel of Learning.*

Line 13: *"takes . . . decision."* Louis Dudek: "poetry . . . must . . . take the risk of a decision"; "to say what we know, loud and clear — and if necessary ugly — that would be better than to say nothing with great skill." "The New Laocöon," *Origin*, Winter – Spring 1956.

Lines 14-15: *"Would . . . all?"* "President Eisenhower Vetoes Farm Compromise [Agricultural Act of 1956]," *New York Times*, April 17, 1956: "We would produce more of certain crops at a time when we need less of them. . . . If natural resources are squandered on crops that we cannot eat or sell, all Americans lose."

Line 19: *Ulysses' companions.* "The Companions of Ulysses," Book Twelve, Fable I, *The Fables of La Fontaine* (The Viking Press, 1954).

Line 22: Mitin (From *la mite*, moth). Odorless, non-toxic product of Geigy Chemical Corporation research scientists (Swiss). *New York Times*, April 7, 1956.

Line 23: *"private . . . shame."* See note for line 13.

Line 27: *"things . . . appear."* Hebrews 11:3.